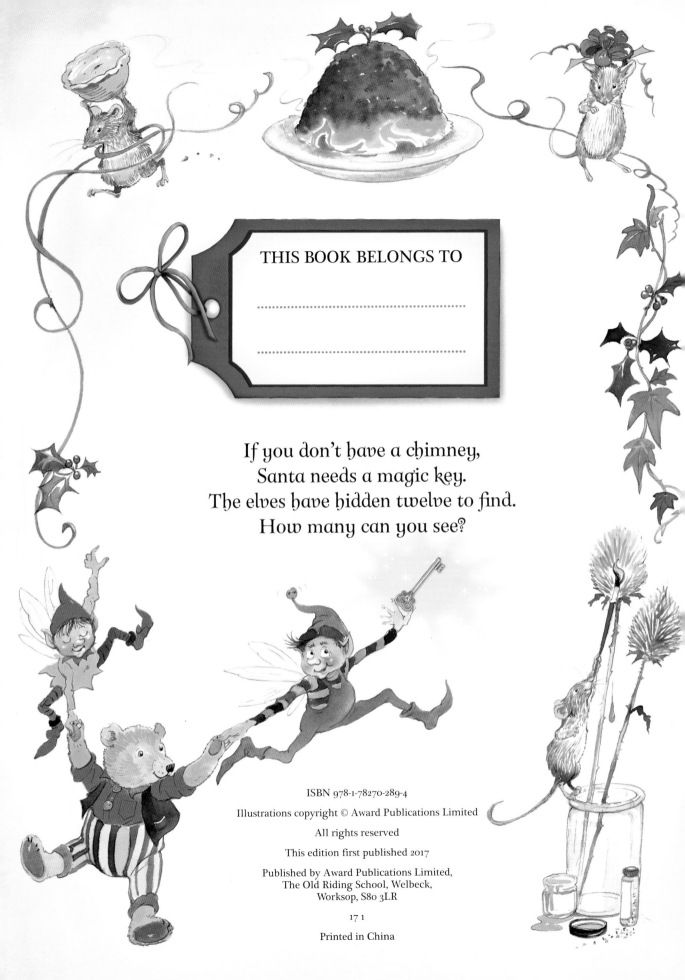

THIS BOOK BELONGS TO

....

....

If you don't have a chimney,
Santa needs a magic key.
The elves have hidden twelve to find.
How many can you see?

ISBN 978-1-78270-289-4

Illustrations copyright © Award Publications Limited

This edition first published 2017

Published by Award Publications Limited,
The Old Riding School, Welbeck,
Worksop, S80 3LR

17 1

Printed in China

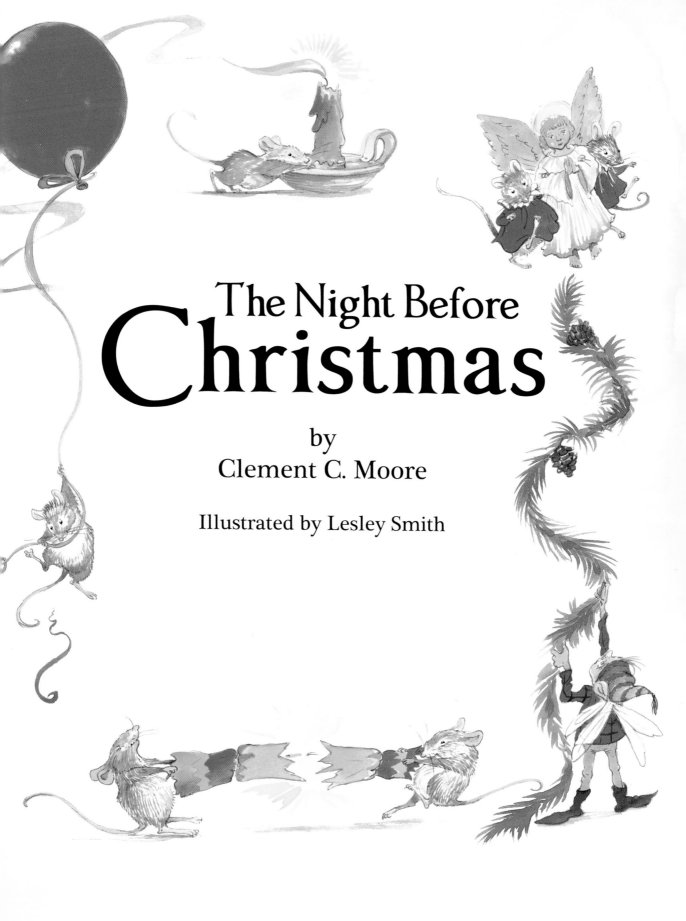

The Night Before Christmas

by
Clement C. Moore

Illustrated by Lesley Smith

AWARD PUBLICATIONS LIMITED

'Twas the night before Christmas,
when all through the house
Not a creature was stirring,
not even a mouse;
The stockings were hung by
the chimney with care,
In hopes that St Nicholas
soon would be there;

The children were nestled
all snug in their beds,
While visions of sugar-plums
danced in their heads;

And Mamma in her kerchief,
and I in my cap,
Had just settled our brains
for a long winter's nap;

When out on the lawn
    there arose such a clatter,
I sprang from the bed
    to see what was the matter.

Away to the window
I flew like a flash,
Tore open the shutters
and threw up the sash.

The moon on the breast
of the new-fallen snow,
Gave lustre of midday
to objects below.

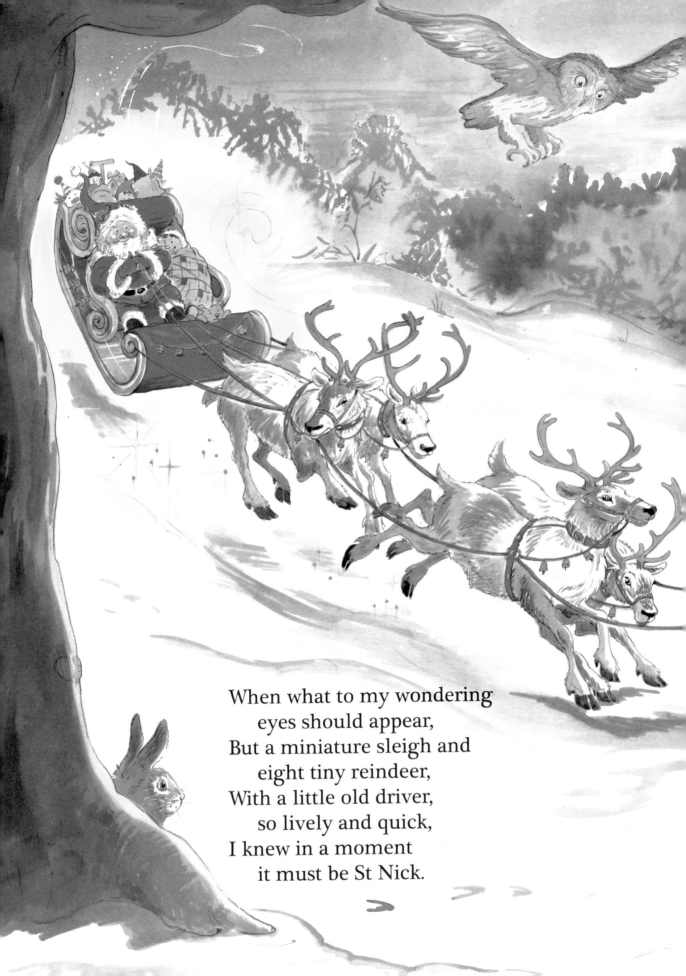

When what to my wondering
        eyes should appear,
But a miniature sleigh and
        eight tiny reindeer,
With a little old driver,
        so lively and quick,
I knew in a moment
        it must be St Nick.

More rapid than eagles
   his coursers they came,
And he whistled and shouted,
   and called them by name:

"Now, Dasher! now, Dancer!
   now, Prancer and Vixen!
On, Comet! on, Cupid!
   on, Donner and Blitzen!

"To the top of the porch,
   to the top of the wall!
Now dash away! dash away!
   dash away all!"
As dry leaves that before
   the wild hurricane fly,
When they meet with an obstacle,
   mount to the sky,
So up to the housetop
   the coursers they flew,
With the sleigh full of toys,
   and St Nicholas too.

And then in a twinkling
I heard on the roof
The prancing and pawing
of each little hoof.
As I drew in my head,
and was turning around,
Down the chimney St Nicholas
came with a bound.

He was dressed all in fur
    from his head to his foot,
And his clothes were all tarnished
    with ashes and soot;

A bundle of toys he had
flung on his back,
And he looked like a pedlar
just opening his pack.

His eyes – how they twinkled!
  his dimples, how merry!
His cheeks were like roses,
  his nose like a cherry!
His droll little mouth
  was drawn up like a bow,
And his beard on his chin
  was as white as the snow.

He had a broad face
    and a little round belly,
That shook, when he laughed,
    like a bowl full of jelly.
He was chubby and plump,
    a right jolly old elf;
And I laughed when I saw him,
    in spite of myself.

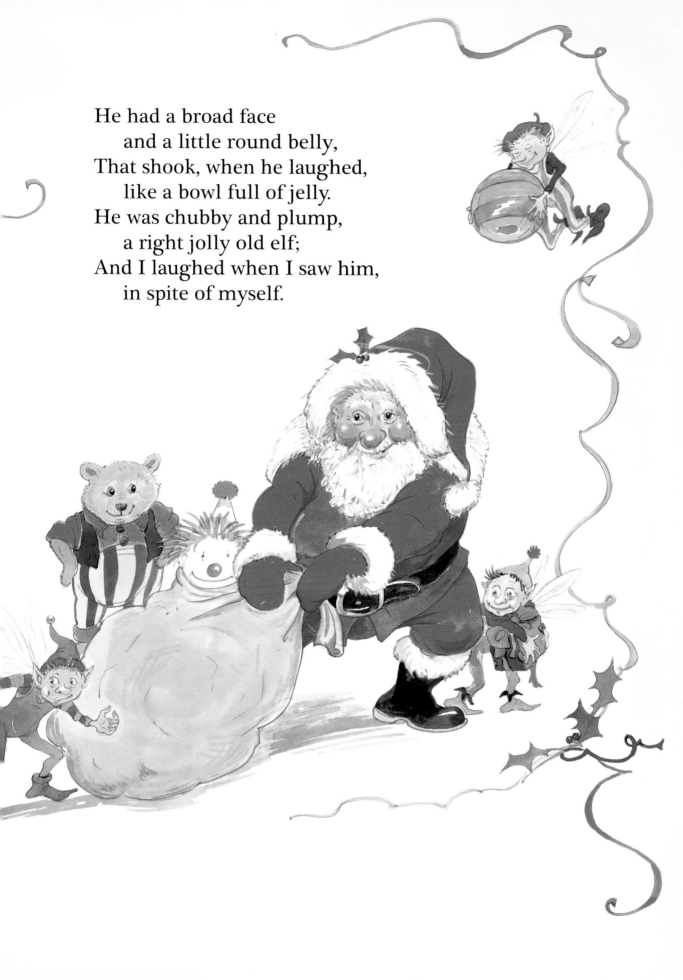

A wink of his eye and a
    twist of his head
Soon gave me to know
    I had nothing to dread.

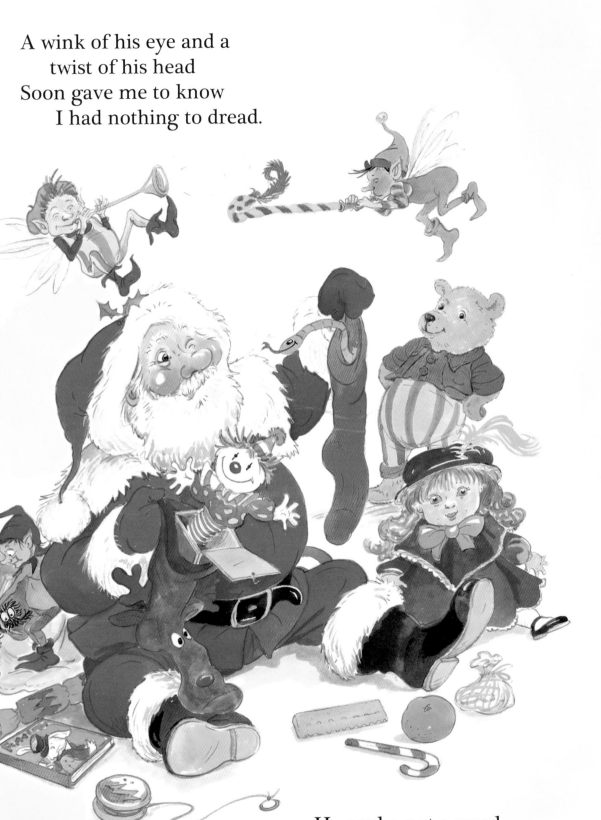

He spoke not a word,
    but went straight to his work,
And filled all the stockings;
    then turned with a jerk.

And laying his finger aside
   of his nose,
And giving a nod, up the
   chimney he rose.

He sprang to his sleigh,
   to his team gave a whistle,
And away they all flew
   like the down of a thistle;

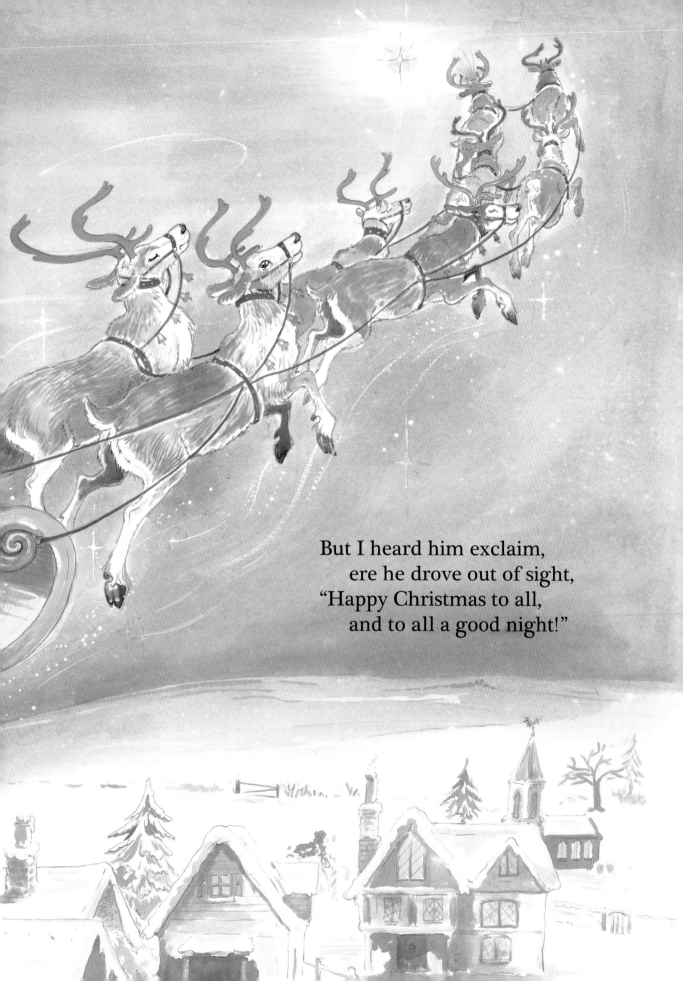

But I heard him exclaim,
    ere he drove out of sight,
"Happy Christmas to all,
    and to all a good night!"